THIS WALKER BOOK BELONGS TO:

_____

_____

_____

YES

Jez Alborough

WALKER BOOKS
AND SUBSIDIARIES
LONDON • BOSTON • SYDNEY • AUCKLAND

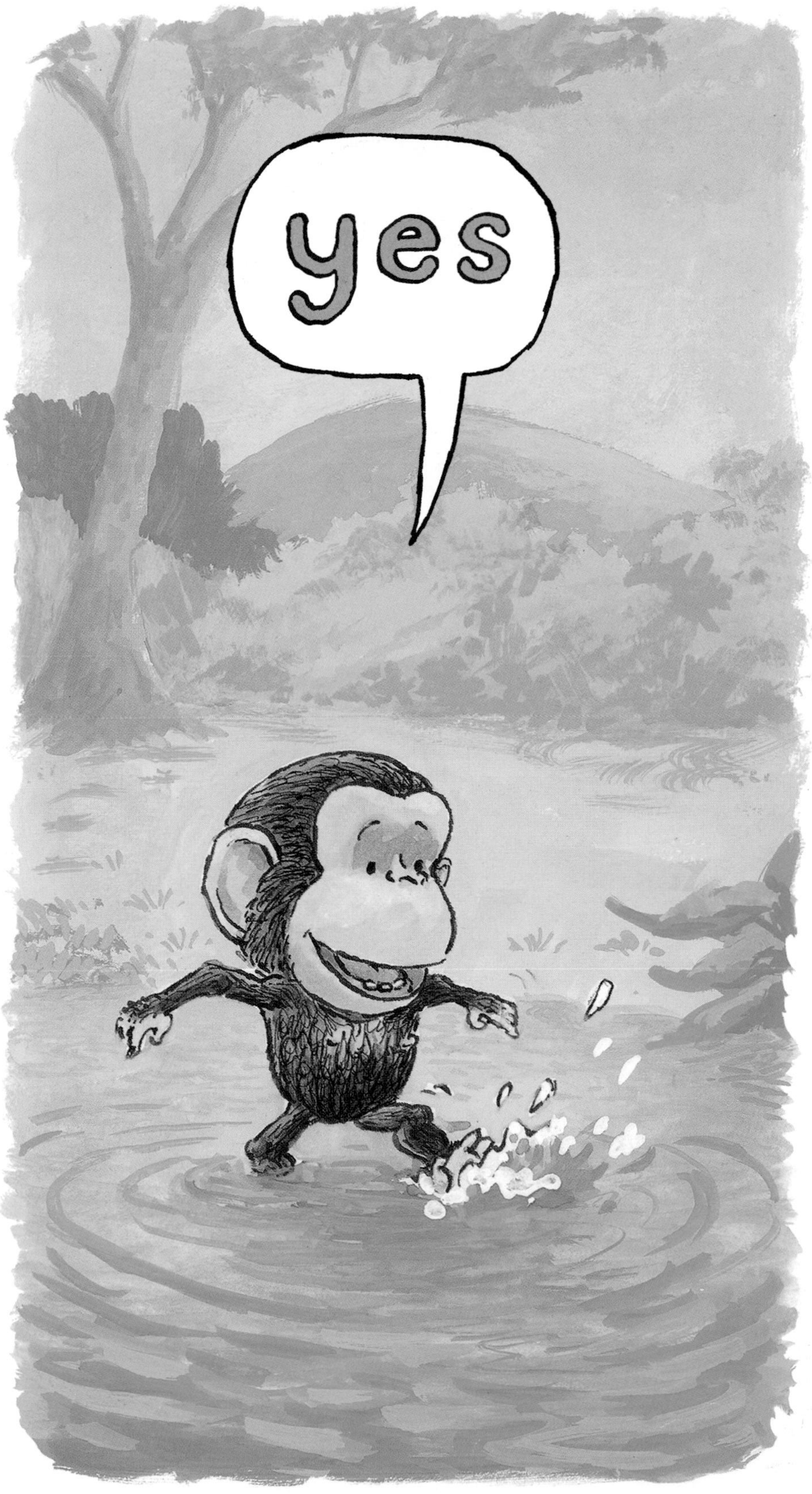
yes

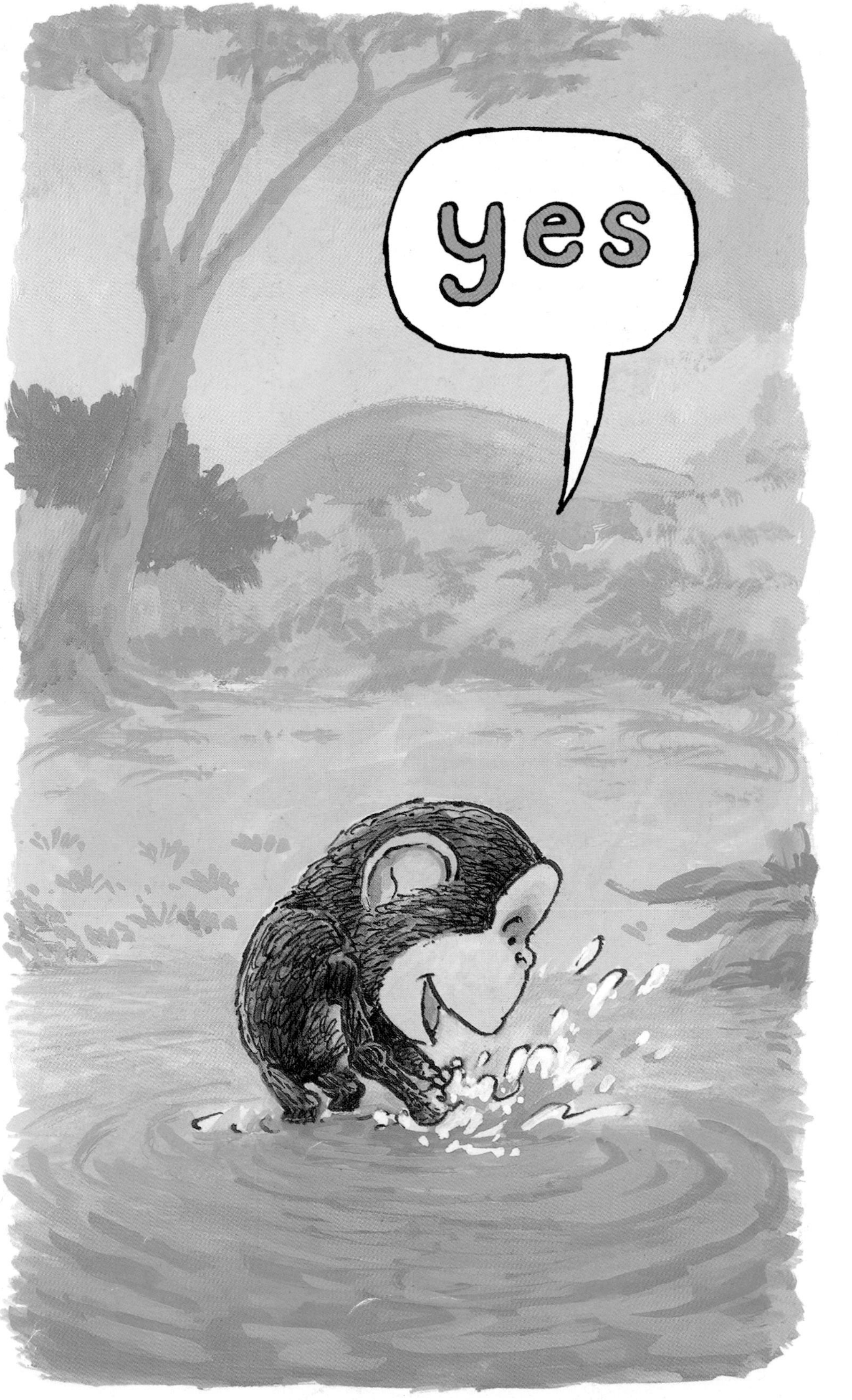
yes

Bobo – the little chimp in the jungle

ISBN: 978-0-7445-8273-4

ISBN: 978-1-4063-0173-1

ISBN: 978-1-4063-0456-5

Hug

All the animals in the jungle have someone to hug – except one little chimp. Will he ever get the hug he needs?

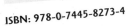

" The big, bright pictures dance off the page with such exuberance that you can't help but feel happy while you are looking at it." Guardian

Tall

Everyone seems to be taller than Bobo. But his friends help him to see that the size you are is the size you're meant to be!

Yes

At Bobo's bath time the little chimp shouts "YES". But at bedtime he cries "NO". It takes two friends and a lot of splashing to turn his "NO" into a "YES".